Golden Moon

A Love & Freedom That's Ours

By Timeless Tate

Edited By Danielle L. Matthews

*A Collection of short stories and poems that centers
Black Queer Romance & Erotica*

Publisher's Cataloging-in-Publication Data

Copyright © 2024 by Timeless Tate

Names: Tate, Timeless, author. |
Matthews, Danielle L., editor.
Title: Golden moon : a love & freedom
that's ours / by Timeless Tate; edited by
Danielle L. Matthews
Description: Baton Rouge, LA: Timeless
Tate, 2025.
Series: Golden Moon

Identifiers: ISBN: 979-8-218-53004-4

Subjects: LCSH African American
women--Fiction. | LGBTQ+ people--
Fiction. | Transgender people--
Fiction. | Romance fiction. | Queer fiction.
| Short stories. | Poetry. | BISAC
FICTION / African American
/ General | FICTION / African American /
Romance | FICTION / Romance /Erotica /
LGBT / Transgender |
FICTION / Southern | FICTION / African
American / Women

Classification: LCC PS3620 .A38 G65
2025 | DDC 813.6--dc23

Table of Contents

Dedication

For all spirits in the universe who dare to love despite everything...again and again. For eternal BLACK sisterhood and BLACK LGBTQ+/Queer communities, and all African descendants both living and ancestral.

Author's Love Letter

Dear Readers,

I want to thank you for taking the time to select and read my body of work. It brings me endless joy to create literary art for the community. All gratitude and blessings to each reader viewing and discussing these stories and poems, hopefully it moved your spirit in some way to share with friends, family, classmates, co-workers, and anyone willing to listen and feel. It took me almost five years to actually sit down and write until completion. The journey of life and the writing process can take its own ownership of time, like most artists know deeply. I welcome you to this collection of work which centers Black Queer Romance & Erotica.

For Liberation and Love,
Your Writer

We Are Beautifully Rebellious

So, they want to silence us?
Just pay it dust.
The more they try to shame us
The more confident and free we become
The more they try to kill us
The more ways we find to live out loud
The more they try to ignore our existence
The more luminous and outspoken we become
The more laws and policies they make to hold us down
The more of us, RISE to fight in the movement
They fail to realize... you can't put a group of people in
shackles
Whose spirit was designed to be revolutionary
Authentic and visionary
Look around, our resilience has spoken, and listen to the
people...our community.

Never Fear...
The more we endure
The more we'll prevail,
Old tales say we're divine treasures,
Stolen secrets,
we've been the Holy Grail,
A living affirmation,
The representation, for
all to transcend

and set sail
The bar for elevation, reincarnation,
and…
Metamorphosis
So miraculous
We Are Beautifully
Rebellious!

The Cat Eyes of Lincoln Drive

A Black & Brown Queer Erotica

She sat on the edge of the bed rubbing oil on her legs, while the bedroom window gave way to the moonlight that was shining down on her ebony skin. Her black cat, Midnight, lays on the window seal watching the moon above while keeping her eyes also on Larissa. Larissa began to move towards the bathroom to get dressed for the big night. Midnight watched her pace back and forth for a while until her phone beeped with a notification. Larissa grabs the phone to read the text message and hears the voice note from Tevin.

On my way - the text message reads.

Tevin sings off-key from the car "It's our anniversary, it's our anniversaaaaaary! I love you girl! On my way. Ayye look though, don't have me waiting 20 years to leave, you already know you look good in anything. Alright, see ya."

Larissa smiles and continues to slide on her lace panties. She reaches for her new black dress that highlights her shape and cleavage, which she managed to snag during an online sale weeks ago. She slips on the dress and then applies her lipstick and earrings. She looks in the mirror and feels damn good about this outfit choice. The black cat sees her walk out the room and return with a box of sex toys and places it on the king-size bed. As if to get prepared for tonight's late-night activities. She knows that they rarely even use them, but she figured tonight should be special right?

A few minutes later, Tevin walks into the apartment with a bouquet of roses and champagne, while Larissa sits on the living room couch. Her brown eyes sparkle and light up in excitement.

"Okaaay, look at you! This is so sweet. Thanks, baby. And you say you don't have a romantic bone in your body." Larissa says embracing him with a hug and kiss.

"Ya know, tonight I gotta switch it up and celebrate us, more importantly you! And look at cho' fine ass. Beautiful as always." Tevin says as he takes in her body in that dress.

"Alright, let me grab my watch off the nightstand and then we can pop open this champagne!" Tevin says kissing her before rushing off towards their bedroom.

Tevin noticed the box on the bed and smiled, shaking his head. He slid on his watch and sprayed his favorite cologne that Larissa bought him last Christmas.

He saw himself in the mirror and was cool with it. He walked back toward the living room grabbing the champagne bottle off the TV stand near Larissa. He poured their glasses and as Larissa reached to grab hers, she somehow knocked the glass all over herself. Her clumsiness chose tonight of all the nights to show up. Champagne spilled all over her dress.

"Nooooo! Fuck! Not my new dress!" Larissa seethes, angrily. She took a big sigh and felt like tonight's sexy look was over and ruined.

"Aww baby, it's okay. It's okay. I got you." Telvin aims to console her in her disappointment while rushing to the kitchen for a towel.

"Ugh! It's no use baby, this shit is ruined now. Thanks though." Larissa was still frustrated but appreciative of Telvin's helpfulness.

"Well, maybe you still got this. Don't you have other dresses in the clost..." Telvin's says while he is interrupted by meowing from Midnight.

Out of nowhere, the black cat walks down the hallway with a red dress in her mouth, her calm purple eyes bright. They both look at each other raising their eyebrows in amazement.

"What the fuck?! How she even know you needed a dress? Ain't that the old dress from way back? See right there. I told you this cat you got from the store, got voodoo powers or some shit." Tevin says weirded out while watching the cat closely.

"Yeah, that was…um ... weird. But maybe she heard me in distress and thought to grab my old dress. That's all, she's just looking out for me. Right? "Larissa says downplaying the unique moment but still appreciative. She grabs the red dress and rubs Midnight's head and body. They hear Midnight's deep purring.

"Well that's solved I guess, let me slide this on. Don't we have reservations?" Larissa asked while squeezing into the dress, Midnight sat below her observing.

"Yeah, we do. Plus, it's a new spot 30 mins across town. You gon like it." Tevin says with pride of his choice and ready to eat.

"Okay, I'm excited...I'm ready... Let's go." Larissa says, smiling and eager.

Midnight watched them leave out the front door. Their perfume and cologne lingered in the air for a while, a light scent that Midnight enjoyed sometimes. Three hours later they returned home with their hands all over each other, kissing. Tevin removed Larissa's dress, exposing her red lace bra and panties. Tevin carries her to the bedroom, laying her on the bed. Midnight can tell they're in heat... and she likes it.

***

Passionate soft moans were coming from the candle-lit bedroom, as the black cat watched the two naked ebony bodies through her purple eyes. The black cat slowly moved to a dark corner inside the bedroom, still transfixed on the woman's body as she received pleasure. The rhythm of the moans, the pace of her breath, and even the way the candlelight flickered across their warm brown skin caused her to purr softly. Tevin himself took his time sliding deep inside her, slow and steady strokes in her voluptuous ass. As the cat gazed, she saw Larissa gripping the bed sheets, biting her bottom lip. She was now in a deeper zone than before, as Tevin sucked on her toes and kissed down her oiled legs, never missing a beat of his stroke and focus.

"Fuck, yes, ahhh, yes!" Larissa says deep in the essence of their rhythm.

"Uhhmm, you like that, don't ya?" Tevin says smoothly in his baritone voice.

Tevin, to her surprise, slowly pulls out of her, and slowly lets her leg go, and moves down to his knees on the floor. He notices she is a little taken aback by this and gives her reassurance to go with the flow.

"Imma try something new, okay? I got you." As he looks down between her legs.

He slowly kissed her thighs moving each kiss higher and higher until he reached her belly. Larissa looks down as he kisses her and thinks for a moment what he might plan to do? She had a feeling but was unsure because if she thinks what she thought he might do, it would not only be something new but her secret desire that finally came to reality!

"Are you sure, because I know this is…." she asks slowly as he continues to kiss all over her body moving down to her center. He whispers "shhhhh" to her, after his last kiss.

He teases her and starts kissing her belly again, moving upward towards her breast. Kissing and licking her areolas. Taking his time savoring her and holding her closely as he remains on his knees.

Their brown bodies created small droplets of sweat, especially around the top of her forehead near her red-colored locs, which he now caresses softly as he sucks on her nipples, and starts nibbling on her full breast. Making a loud sucking sound, as he glances up to look at her face. Confirming her satisfaction he grabbed her thighs sliding her to a lying position. As Tevin grips her thighs he simultaneously opens her legs wider, to gain full access to his sweet treat. He kisses her soft thighs until he reaches her lovestick. He slowly starts sucking on the top of her penis, allowing his warm long tongue to go in circles around and around in his mouth. Tevin then slides her deeper into his mouth. As he does so, he looks up from his treat to meet her gaze then he gives her a sexy wink as he begins to devour her. She is in total shock and she can feel her precum starting to drip out for him.

She's actually in disbelief right now! Tevin has said time and again "I like all kinds of women, but I don't do that freaky gay shit." It was so annoying for Larissa to hear people categorize her sex as a woman with men as "gay shit" especially from her own man.

She agrees her unique lived experience was surely complex and different. She also resolved that loving Tevin meant she would have to forego certain pleasures including oral sex. But she loved him and was willing to make the sacrifice. Today, at this moment, she was so happy that he would love her more fully. She knew topping him was definitely out of the question. Before tonight, Tevin always ignored her penis in bed. Many of the girls who date straight men deal with this. While other straight men love to play with a lady's penis, with no problem. Regardless, with all the money and love he gives her on a regular basis, she was gladly ready to be taken care of and let this sex position go out the window. Tonight though, he seems to be in a new light or mood to spice things up. Larissa gives herself permission and surrenders to all the glory of his mouth and tongue tonight.

Tevin continued to suck on her, his head moving up and down as he caressed her thighs. He moved his huge brown hands to her butt, slowly squeezing it. As he slowly lets her penis slide out his mouth, Tevin allows a little slob to drip on her tip. He then licks his index and second fingers and slides those warm, wet fingers into her soft pulsating pink anus. Tevin fingered Larissa in a smooth motion in and out and all around, while he moves back to suck her again. With all this happening, Larissa's mind is foggy with pleasure. She's in her pleasure zone and can feel Tevin's tongue circling her penis and the flow of his big fingers inside her sweet tunnel. The combination was driving her crazy as her eyes rolled to the back of her head. Larissa's hips gyrated forward and backward and in small circles as her heart pounded in her chest, she could not keep up with her breaths. Tevin could feel Larissa's penis expanding in his mouth, almost like a small balloon.

Larissa's climax was so close. Sensing this, Tevin sucked harder and moved his head around in circular motions, allowing his mouth to completely be filled.

"Ahh, ohh'' bab..baby. Ahh, right there ouu, right there ." Larissa whined and moaned. She felt his mouth taking over her penis and devouring her.

Larissa was nearing her end! She couldn't take any more, she was ready. Tevin saw Larissa wiggle again. She tried to push Tevin's head back in case he was cum averse. Tevin was new to sucking a lovestick and Larissa didn't want to spoil the experience by releasing it in his mouth without consent. She wanted him to do this many more times to come! Tevin said he was down to spice things up, one giant step was enough, but he wasn't ready to swallow her cum. He allowed her to move his mouth away from her penis. Larissa took her penis in her hand pointing her erection straight at Tevin. He moved closer to allow her to lay her penis on his muscular brown chest. As she climaxed releasing her juices all over his pecs and continued to pulsate.

The thick cream slowly ran down his chest to his belly, slowly moving though his stumble black chest hair. With a droplet of cum also landed on his beard. His ebony chest was glazed with her cream, like a warm donut. He pulled her closer and hugged her tightly as her body continued to convulse, she held him tightly tensing her grasp with each aftershock. She ran her wet sticky fingers up and down gently caressing his muscular back. He was at ease and enjoyed their joint body heat as he held her. Tevin was still on his knees as Larissa moved to a seated position on the edge of the bed. They both stayed like this for a few moments, breathing hard and waiting for their heart rates to return to normal. Tevin, clearly aroused, took his free hand and began to rub on his dick. Larissa, who felt his arm moving, lifted his face and started passionately kissing him as he stroked himself. Tevin rose up, pushing Larissa back on the bed to bestride her in missionary, using his thighs to keep both of her legs open he slid inside her shuttering as her body gripped around his dick. Larissa let out a moan as Tevin stroked and pounded her pleasure center until he climaxed in sweaty delight.

The black cat recognized this as her moment to exit the room. The lovers gazing in each other's eyes fixating on their passion filled night. Midnight took one last look at the couple, her purple eyes gleaming in the candle light, but dim enough not to distract the two lovers. Larissa, though, could see from far away in the corner of her eye, a long black tail moving out the room. She made a mental note, to lock the bedroom door whenever she and Tevin were engaged in intimate moments because who has time for Midnight to be walking back and forth, leaving fur all around when she's getting fucked down. Nope.

* * *

In the morning, Midnight was lying in her cat bed near the living room window. The sunlight peeking through the blinds gave hues of gold and orange mixture. She turned her head toward the sound of the bedroom door opening, where she saw Larissa in her plush white robe and slippers in pursuit of her breakfast, waffles and strawberries. Tevin managed to roll out of bed and walk toward their hallway to grab a towel from the linen closet. He heads straight to the bathroom where he runs the shower. They both were in their morning solitude in separate areas, in their own world. The home was peaceful now the way Midnight liked it sometimes, before the commotion of human hustle and bustle. There was a sense of calmness in the air, so much so, Midnight began to drift back into a nap. As she snuggled in her cat bed she heard a faint scraping of floor wood above her. Midnight could hear the sounds of the neighbors when the house was quiet like this. Faint squeaking noises came from the upstairs unit. She was curious so she left her bed to investigate. She noticed Larissa looking up at the ceiling, rolling her eyes at the noise and turned on some R&B music.

Midnight swiftly walked towards the cat entrance of their back door, which leads to the apartment stairwell. She climbed the stairway to see through her neighbor's window. The blinds were open halfway, allowing her to see perfectly. Midnight saw a sight that was slightly strange or new to her. She never saw a woman in this standing position before, doing what she was doing. Midnight's eyes sparked as she watched the tan body move back and forth…she was thrusting.

A woman with a Spanish accent spoke to another woman, they both were naked. Carmen had one hand on the woman's ass and another one pulling on her long dark silky hair. There was a poster of the pioneering Mexican painter Frida Kahol, hanging over their bed wall. The women thrusting and moving back and forth, causes one of their lavender pillows to drop softly on the floor.

"More…ahh…more,.. Ahh deeper baby!" said Maria in a heated Spanish accent who was bent over in doggy style.

Carmen, who had a muscular manish frame to her, continued and obeyed the order, and slid her strap-on deeper inside Maria, causing her to moan and get wetter. Her pink flower oozes with cream around the woman's long black pipe. Carmen pulls the strap-on out of Maria's pussy, revealing all the slippery sauce from their fucking. Carmen with a strong body frame sported a tattoo on her neck and was wearing a loose basketball cap that allowed some of her luscious dark brown hair to fall down her back. Carmen licks her fingers and rubs her wet fingers on Maria's pink wet pussy lips. She bends down to kiss Maria's butt cheek, then heads to the labia using her tongue to stoke back and forth. Carman kissed her clit, the sensation made Maria moan deeply. Carmen continued to sink her tongue and face into the woman's pussy, going wild now, as love liquid started to smear over Carmen's face. Carmen drank her honey while still keeping her eyes on Maria's tan supple booty.

Carmen was eating her out so deep, that Midnight thought Maria's ass might swallow the woman whole. The only visible thing was the neck tattoo. The two women were both in a heated ecstasy and ready for full force. The tattooed woman gilded her hand underneath Maria's thigh, and raised her up, cupping her thighs around her neck and Carmen was standing up while Maria sat on her shoulders, as she continued savoring her pussy. Maria felt her walls clinching and she began to shake uncontrollably. Maria shouted a cry-like moan and released all her honey onto the woman's face. The woman went full throttle, going reckless, as cum leaked over Carmen's face and neck, like a tiger devouring a watermelon.

Midnight purred at the sight of their lustful delight.

* * *

The sun was now hovering brightly over the city, as it started to warm the metal of the terrace. Midnight could feel the metal's heat under her black paws. There was another sound, just as faint as the last one, coming from under her. Something shifted in the air as she moved quietly down each step to the lower floor. It sounded like a human crying from apartment A9. The apartment window was wide open, where she noticed the humming of a cordless fan near a pile of clothes. The room was dark and the apartment was oldly warm with heat escaping the window. As Midnight got closer to sit, she saw two Black men holding each other in the center of the bed. The two had a bucket of ice in the bed with them. One of the guys grabs an ice cube and rubs it across his chest for a second of coolness, then shares it with Marcus, rubbing it on his forehead. There was a moment of silent tenderness between them that lingered, until one of the guys' tears left his eyes and ran down his face, now mixing with the sweat from their mahogany bodies. They lay facing the wall near a nightstand that had stacks of envelopes on it. The envelopes had large red words on them that read "Late Notice." Something that Midnight remembers seeing in her past with Larissa, that seems to always bring her to take a deep sigh. Andre started to kiss Marcus ' shoulder while caressing him to bring some sort of comfort in the messy space they were in. Andre turned over to him, kissing Marcus while tears were still in his eyes.

One of their voices emerges from the room.

"We gon make it through this, you hear me? We gon be alright." as one of the men says in sure certainty.

Midnight could sense the feelings of sadness and exhaustion from the humans in the room. A deep agony that never should mix with the summer heat. She wished she could bring some sort of soothing solace for them.

But instead, the curious cat decided to mind her business for once and move on home.

Giving these two the space for privacy and being.

* * *

Midnight hurried back upstairs to her living room. She saw a glimpse of Larissa in an office dress, pouring her some cat food for today. Midnight was pleased and meowed at Larissa to say thank you. Larissa walks over to the window seal where Midnight sat looking. Larissa gave her a warm pet and rubbed her down to the end of her tail causing Midnight to purr softly again, to the touch of her home friend.

"Have a good day Midnight. Listen now, don't scratch up anything while I'm gone," Larissa says as she looks down at Midnight as her eyes glisten bright purple from the sunlight.

She pets and embraces her again, picks up the lint roller from the table by the door then heads out of the door to work.

The place was peaceful again. Midnight could hear and tell the apartment was empty due to no sound of snoring, walking, the smell of weed, or sounds of rap music that Telvin often played. He must have left for work too, before Larissa today. Midnight decided to stretch her body out on the wooden floor, and allow her black fur to catch some warm summer light through the window. Midnight could always see from the window, the old apartment leasing office sign that read "Welcome to Lincoln Drive Apartments'.

She closed her eyes and slowly drifted off to sleep, in hopes of another catnap...or wet dream.

Rising

I'm Rising
I'm Rising
I'm Rising

Making self changes
Breaking these chains
Learning new ways
Steps in a better direction
Affirming my days

I'm Rising
I'm Rising
I'm Rising

Finally started forgiving
Healing past pains
Leaving the struggle and heaviness away
Shining through old shame
Shedding the anchor of heartbreak, poverty,
stolen ideas.

I'm Rising
I'm Rising
I'm Rising

Doing the best I can with the time I have,

Sometimes stumbling but still walking
Deep breath and exhale…serenity
Enlightening my course and humanity

I'm Rising
I'm Rising
I'm Rising

No longer in my own way
Savoring the blessings
I'm growing lighter
Feeling less sadder
Flying higher
Golden paths for rest of my days

I'm Rising
I'm Rising
I'm Rising

Like a Black panther in the night, I rose.

When Love Continues...

A Black Queer Spiritual Romance

The summer breeze blew a butterfly that grazed her brown legs as she sat gazing at the cemetery. She turned to see where the butterfly was flying and smiled as she noticed the children playing at the local park a few blocks away. She rose off the bench holding her flowers tightly in her hand. The wind began to blow her white dress as she bent down to lay the flowers on her husband's final resting place. She took a deep breath, exhaled softly, and touched the marble tombstone; in that moment, miraculous peace fell over her and the world became heavenly still. She instinctively knew today was special, as it had always been for years, she could sense it in the air and cosmos. She smiled and decided to head home to take a rest...to be ready.

Later that night, as she sat on the bed, the house was soothingly quiet. She knew tonight was the night. She walked to the dining room table that she decorated nicely with fancy plates and silverware, pure white candles, and a portrait of him…in the center of the table. She baked a vanilla birthday cake earlier that day for the occasion. She decided to sit down near the window and wait. Luna saw the luminous full moon hovering over the city, and she smiled.

She looked at the living room clock that hung on the wall, which read 11:59 pm, then turned her attention to the rocking chair in the corner of the room. She gazed and slowly the rocking chair began to rock, swinging in a smooth familiar rhythm, back and forth. She smiled big, becoming anxious like a young schoolgirl. The chair stopped rocking, and then suddenly…he appeared.

"Hey baby, I hope you weren't staying up all night waiting on me." He said while walking towards her with a smile, his dark brown skin glistening, long crown locs hanging like wool ropes, and his baritone voice welcoming.

"Chile please, I got better things to do than sit up waiting for you," Luna replied, rolling her eyes and flirting. He kissed her on the lips and that kiss sent chills down her spine, electric sparks of pure joy.

"You don't have to keep doing this for me, you know Luna." He said, pointing out.

"I know Charles, but it's still your birthday and I only get this moment once every 5 years. I will never stop celebrating." She said strongly almost as a promise to the universe and herself.

Charles smiled at her unwavering strength and devotion, something that never changed throughout their lifetimes.

"I think I already know, but I still want to ask you. How are you feeling, baby?" Charles asks, sitting down close to her.

"Honestly, just managing. Somewhere in between letting it flow again and still tired. But your brother on the other hand." Luna says in retrospection.

"Yeah, I figure you felt that way. This time is going to be different, I can feel it. But, what's been going on with Kelvin lately? You spoke to him?" Charles asked.

"Yeah, he calls from time to time, checking on me and making sure I'm okay with you being gone. You know he told me once, that he still calls your phone just to hear your voice on the voicemail. He's checking on me, but baby I think he's taking it the hardest of anyone." She says resting her head on his shoulder.

"I had a feeling. That's my baby brother though! We were thick as thieves, and I know he misses me." Charles said as he continued caressing through her coarse hair. "Just keep being there for him Luna, you are the only living thing left that's a connection to me that he has."

"I know, I will. Maybe you should visit him for a chance. He might love that." She said to Charles.

"Nah. I turned the TV on once when he was home alone to give him a signal, he got really nervous. He's not ready yet for a visit. I don't want to scare him or get him weirded out." Charles said in retrospection.

"Yeah, let's not do that then. Wait, was that you helping me last week when I mistakenly left my keys in the car and the door out of nowhere just unlocked?" Luna asked, recalling the moment.

"Yes! That was me, stepping in to help you. But, baby, I told you a thousand times to get a spare key and that you can't keep rushing for work in the morning like that." Charles says laughingly.

"Listen, you know I have a hard time keeping up with those material things. I figured it was you. Look at my husband coming through for me…still." She said happily. Luna looked out the window and noticed that the position of the moon had shifted in the sky as time passed.

"We don't have much longer till sunrise," Luna says with a familiar sadness creeping in on her.

"Baby don't look like that. I'm going nowhere really. We are soulmates, like literally." Charles says, trying to cheer her up.

"Charles, but each time we do this it's both beautiful and bittersweet! It's so frustrating how each time we fall in love you have to die young which leaves me to grow old alone each generation and lifetime. It's still heartbreaking not having you here physically throughout the days. I'm so happy we decided not to have children this time around. I couldn't go through

another incarnation with my babies asking about
their late father, you missing important
moments in their adult lives, and having them
grieve over you with that look in their eyes on
Father's Day. I can't keep doing this so-called
living and moving on without you." Luna finally
stated with tears falling as she gazed longingly
into Charles' eyes.

"Aww, baby come here. I know, I know.
These lives we had were never easy for us, we
just keep figuring out each life, new body, new
religion, and new generation we are born into. I
hear you when you say you're tired of this cycle
and me leaving too soon."Charles said,
connecting to her pain. Then he continued trying
to console her. "Do you remember how nervous
we both were about you transitioning? I'm still
shocked you were assigned male at birth! Goes
to show we never know what body we'll get in
any lifetime." Charles says reminiscing.

"You were shocked? Try knowing all
along your spirit is different than the body you
were born with and everybody saying you're
crazy or sinful for expressing yourself like a
girl; having that constant frustration with the
world othering you; and, going on with this
inner knowing, while outsiders continue
clouding you with their beliefs. But one thing is
for sure, I always had you by my side to help me

through those transitioning years. Protecting and loving me through it." Luna says, remembering her metamorphosis.

"I was so pissed off when your parents kicked you out of the house for dressing as a girl and identifying as transgender. I knew then like I've always known, I love you and always will.

Baby, we were fearless back then. We packed our bags, drove to the next big town, landed some odd jobs, and lived in motels until I could afford a decent apartment for us. We were determined to make it and rise. No doubt, we lived, each lifetime." Charles says proudly.

Luna looks off into the distance and then looks back at him with a serious look, she is ready to get something off her chest. "Baby I'm glad we lived and all, like it's truly a gift to have these memories, but my spirit is exhausted! I have seen things and even survived things that are just too much. I don't want to keep living again and again. I don't know anymore if I want to keep doing this." Luna says, staring into Charles' eyes with certainty.

"Maybe you don't have to. That's why I want to talk to you this time about something serious." Charles announced while holding her hands as she looked up at him in curiosity.

"What are you talking about?" Luna inquired breathlessly.

"I've been thinking about the fate of our love. Let's stay among the ancestors forever and become guardian angels for other humans. Let's finally reach the highest ascension." Charles says as he looks serious and nervous about Luna's response.

"But...wait. Can we even do that? We can't decide that, right? We have been living and dying, rebirthing as a couple since Ancient Africa. Plus, how do you know God says we've finished our mission on earth yet?" Luna asked in astonishment.

"My love, we have been on this earth for centuries. I'm sure we've learned enough and provided enough service to humanity in our human bodies. So, let's elevate to living in the spiritual realm. All we have to do is ask God." Charles says in cool serenity.

The sun began to slowly appear, giving a glow of light over the horizon. They knew the visit was coming to an end, but they both believed in a new journey. A rebirth of love in a new realm.

"So, what do you think, Luna? Come with me and let's go home." Charles states as he slowly fades getting lighter and lighter, becoming translucent.

"Baby, you're fading away. Yes, of course, I'll go with you, but when? When do I transcend? How long do I have on earth this time?!" Luna asked swiftly.

"You know I can't tell you that, but just know I'm waiting for you on the other side. Keep living, keep laughing, and take care of yourself. I'm always right here, right next to you. No more visiting, because our spirits are going to stay with God this time around. I love you, Luna." Charles says as he walks towards the sunlight in the window, slowly fading into the guiding light above.

She sighed and took a deep breath. Watching him leave each time was always an ocean of emotions. An echoing farewell, that hadn't softened as time passed. Just left remnants of shadows within the mind. Resemblance of a beloved photograph swept by the waves of a shore. A sense of sadness and completeness swelled up within her. Even a mixture of feelings of both abandonment and omnipresence from Charles. His departure has always cut deep to her core. Crystalizing her solitude with endlessness and herself.

His departure also made her reflect on her lives. This living she was doing was heavy. She remembered images of her as a little girl staring distraught at the sight of her father lynched from a Spanish moss tree, which grew gray moss that forever etched grey clouds in the reclusive chambers of her soul. A permanent stain that carried over all her next lives, giving the reason why she never liked Spanish moss trees. They triggered unbearable glimpses of the past. She remembered way back in Africa the heat of the sun and cool sands of the Nile River. Her mind ventured to another life on the Atlantic coastline where she could distinctly hear the native tongue of Yoruba women from her village speaking in groups freely, a form of liberation on unconquered, non-colonized soil and land.

"Alafia, eyin arabinrin mi. Bawo ni o?"

(Peace, my sisters. How are you?)

Unfortunately, she also remembered attending her brother's funeral after World War II and only a few months later the traumatic night when her last mother, in her previous life, died in her arms unexpectedly on a mundane day. Witnessing firsthand the woman that gave her life now transitioning and entering the spiritual plane, after her mother's last breath.

The familiarity of death was like an old song ringing in her head from a broken jukebox she so dreadfully wanted to throw out the nearest window. Too many eulogies she had to endure always being the last one to grow old. She felt her very being getting tired again, a sensation that never left, just muted the humming occasionally, on a good day.

***

Later that day, rays of afternoon sunlight began to enter the house. She could see out the window her many neighbors; one family barbequing in the backyard, a woman gardening on the side of her house, a bunch of elders playing cards on the porch, and a small group of girls playing jump rope with adorable pigtails and box braids. She cherished the sight of black folks just living. In the living room where she sat were photos of her in gold frames from childhood through adulthood. Some with her former body as a child and some now as her true self, the feminine embodiment of today. She sat there for a while in deep reflection. She thought of her life presently and the repeated lives she lived over the centuries. She had many careers, birthed children, learned different languages, traveled, felt both the privilege of wealth and oppression of poverty, and attended many parties and ceremonies in so many lives, but the most sacred to her was the blessing of having true everlasting love with Charles. Having Charles to spend each life with, to connect and relate to, was the medicine to her soul and the treasure of her lives.

As she sat, she began to feel moments capsulized in her mind. Luna began traveling through past events. This often happened minutes, or hours, after Charles transitioned on. She knew what to do. She allowed it to rise up, to the surface, and begin playing out in herself.

The Year 1927

She could hear the saxophone playing from the outside area of the dance hall. He held her hand firmly as she slowly walked up the stairs wearing her red satin dress that sculpted her body sultrily. The room was filled with electrifying people from around town. People were dancing, drinking, and smoking; some were paired sitting at tiny tables alongside the walls. It was one of the main spots in the city where coloreds could mingle, unwind, and break free after a long work week. Many parts were segregated, but this was all ours to claim, this place a sanctuary of blackness, a Black oasis within a public space to call home. Things were on the brink of change from years earlier, the colored folks were speaking of a new age of art and expression for us. Whatever the people were calling it, she for sure felt the excitement in the air tonight.

After dancing for a while, Ava saw an empty table with a small red candle near a window giving a view of the city's night lights. She swayed to the chair, giving a wink to Darrion, as a gush of smoke from surrounding cigars lingered in the air, but he caught sight of her alluring eyes as she walked away. He ordered drinks for two, and walked towards the woman that had always owned a presence… that was pulling him in closer. He sat across from her, as she smiled, with light sweat near her temples. He also had tiny beads of sweat from dancing and was perfectly fine with it.

"Oh baby, I haven't danced like that in a minute. Look at this place, it's so alive." Ava says catching her breath.

"I know, this atmosphere is on fire. I'm glad I had time to bring you here tonight. I also want to share something with you while we're here." Darrion says.

Ava looked up from the glass she was sipping with curiosity and concern "Yes Darrion, I'm listening."

"I'm not sure if I have shown it enough lately with me working long hours on the railroad. I want you to know, that I honor and cherish your existence. I take this journey and our union sacred. I know I have been silent in my head at times, but I see you and appreciate you for everything. For all the lives we've lived, children we've raised, and countless times we shared." He said in pure sincerity.

"Darrion, you don't have to worry about saying it, you show me just in your presence. I know you cherish us and what we have." Ava said, ensuring him that his love never went blind, dull, nor unfelt, no matter how hard his workload or how long his moments of silence.

She was more concerned with the real issue, how colored folks had to work so hard, backbreaking for what seemed like pennies. What's heartbreaking was seeing that wear and tear on his body in this lifetime. From a high chief back in Africa, only a few hundred years ago, to an industrial worker here in America. That dichotomy was unsettling. Something she never mentioned due to the joy he found in providing for them, and the realities of employment for coloreds.

He sat back in the seat for a second and took in the setting. "You know most men would have given you a ring or some silly sentimental thing for this type of moment. But I know ain't nothing can materialize this right here." Darrion announced.

"Hmm baby you're right, so just keep giving me…you." She said while staring intensely into his eyes, now rubbing her finger and tracing the rim of the glass.

Darrion could feel her flirtatious nature and knew to lean into it. He looked around the place where there were paintings on the wall, many colored folks in their best dressed from fancy dresses to tailored suits dancing under the main chandelier that hung from the ceiling.

"This place may be beautiful tonight, but my eyes are on you. You look divine." Darrion said.

"Oh, do I just look it, or am I divine?" She said to him with a flick of her eyes shimmering, teasing him. She remembered that regardless of the body he had, his spirit always enjoyed her moments of intimate teasing.

"Oooh, I feel you. Both, baby. All divine" Darion says licking his lips and staring intensely back at her.

He reached over and grabbed her hand, rubbing slowly while they locked eyes. At that moment, the jazz music disappeared and the noise of the room was silenced. It was only them now; space and time were theirs. She felt a pulsating surge through her, an internal flame that happens at times when touching each other and embracing their union. They were now both transfixed on each other. A natural love potion that was created by angels entwining their bond and fate. She could feel him closer now. Coming in for a kiss on her cheek then gently moving to suckle her neck. Soft strokes of his tongue made circles on her skin. He began to smell the fragrance she was wearing. A light scent was only noticeable up close, like he was now.

"Hmmm, you smell good baby." He says softly, still kissing her neck.

"It's vanilla bean." She replies enticingly.

"You know I like the smell and taste of vanilla." He says whispering in her ear.

"Umhhmm, how about we get out of here and you can taste some vanilla for dinner." She said finally whispering back in his ear. She turned her head slightly caressing his earlobe with the curve of her lips and gave a quick nibble. She sent the invitation.

He immediately swung up out of the chair, catching his balance, and rising away from the table. She giggled at the sight of his reflex and still being a source of aphrodisiac after all their years. She grabbed her clutch and they were both ready to leave. They walked towards the door, him holding her waist tenderly. The saxophone continued to serenade the many people in the room, as they drifted out into the night.

Luna slowly came back to the present after daydreaming of the good ole days with Charles. Sweet memories she often recalled whenever she saw paintings or photographs of Harlem, or moments like now, when she simply sat still long enough. She sighed again and decided to light some cannabis herbs and frankincense to give the house aromatherapy and to relax herself.

Her phone rang several times that day, but she never bothered answering it. Although, she felt a strange urge to speak to her loved ones for some reason.

She embraced this moment in time, in her home, where she could always be as naked internally as she saw fit. Here, her blackness, trans-ness, and reincarnated spirit could be released and simply be in this safe space. The shedding and unfolding were all hers naturally. Luna cried that evening tears of joy and inner peace. She could feel herself finally letting go of the burdens of life, thick stones that seem embedded within after centuries of baggage, memories, and lifespans. She felt her being slowly loosening grip on all forms of attachment in the earthly realm. Her essence became lighter, she lifted herself up and like the sun rising continued with her day. She placed her dishes in the sink, took a hot soaking bath, and moisturized her rich melanin skin with cocoa butter lotion. She changed into her loungewear to take a rest. She felt a sense of life after this visit, a sense of new freedom and a new beginning. She decided to allow her big afro to lay free on the pillow and she gazed at the sun through the window blinds. She laid in bed for a while with a smile, then said a prayer and slowly drifted to sleep. That day she exhaled for the final time in a human body… in her final lifetime.

Iridescent

Since the Ancient Egyptian times
We have flourished on this earth and called it
mines
And live brilliantly outside the lines

Although we have been
Kicked out of churches
Forgotten in history
Silenced in politics
Outcast in society
Still like the luminous sun…we rise.

My LGBTQ+ community
My beloved brothers, sisters, and siblings
Black, white, tall, short, skinny, or thick
Take pride in yourselves
Hold your heads high
We are the diamonds in the sky
You are not a mistake, defect, sinner, or
confused
You are amazingly designed
And beautifully divine.

Let's never forget, the trailblazers that came
before us

James Baldwin…Langston Hughes…
Nicki Giovanni
Frances Thompson…Bayard Rustin…
Alvin Ailey…
Marsha P. Johnson…Crystal LaBeija…
E. Lynn Harris…
Sylvester … Richmond Barthe…
Willmar Broadnax…Jackie Shane
Octavia St. Laurent
And many more of our ancestors.

We are artistic and imaginative
From Architecture to hair
From Literature to Fashion
From Dance to Medicine
We are Human
We are "The People"
We are a community
We are citizens
We are…the colors and shades of liberty that
define America.

Vibrant

A Black Queer Romantic Comedy

"Girl what are you doing" says

Savannah as she sees her friend Lisa walking towards the door of the bar heading to jump in the car with an unfamiliar woman. "What does it look like, I'm leaving," says Lisa straightforwardly.

"Why are you leaving with that lady, you just met her tonight!" Savannah proclaimed. "No, actually I met her online, remember? We have been talking on the phone and texting for weeks now," Lisa said.

"Yeah, but you never even met the woman face to face until tonight, like a hot hour ago!" Savannah says, placing her martini glass on the bar and turning her body to face Lisa. "Look out the window. You see that lady leaning on the Corvette, she is finer than wine. Looking like a full bodied merlot in that red dress and those red heels. You want me to pass that up? I'm hitting that tonight! I don't care if you disapprove cause this girl is about to get hers tonight!" Lisa boldly says to Savannah.

"It's not that I don't want you to have fun. I just want you to be safe because you're moving like you did in your old college days. Hmm" Savannah said with a side-eye. Lisa thought it was shady of her to bring this up now.

"Girl after this rough breakup I need to get under something sexy! And right NOW! And that woman, standing over there, looks like the exact treat I need." Lisa said as both women they both pick up their drinks toasting to Lisa getting her groove back.

"I guess! Live your life then. I do want you to move on, so have fun…like I already know you will. Wait…you got protection, right?" asked Savannah.

"Lesbians don't need condoms." Lisa says, looking shocked that her friend asked something so ridiculous.

"I'm talking about a damn weapon girl. Here's my taser. Use it if you need cause I heard these days even the Lesbians can be serial killers," Savannah said, taking her taser out of her purse to give to Lisa.

"You watch too many mystery movies and crime shows. I'm going to be okay. Plus I'm already strapped so keep your lil taser for yourself." Lisa then continues "Besides I like MY women a little crazy and a lotta feisty," she says jokingly.

"Ugh girl you a mess, bye Lisa! Go have fun. Are you coming to work tomorrow?" asked Savannah.

"Yep, at 8 am promptly. Unless she freaks me so good, I might walk in hella late" Lisa says as she drinks her last shot of alcohol and laughs. "Okay, that's enough, bye Lisa. That's TMI!. Oh, by the way, Lesbians can engage in safer sex too, it's called dental dam! So go buy one fast." Savannah says as Lisa walks out the bar door. Lisa rolls her eyes at Savannah's remark and jumps in the car with the unfamiliar woman.

As Savannah sat there by herself at the bar, she couldn't help but think about her next stage in life. Lisa was living it up with her sex adventures. She was enjoying life. On the flip side Savannah wanted to have kids, but with her busy work schedule and unique love life, there probably wasn't much chance of that anytime soon. Plus, her life wasn't exactly vanilla, so she wasn't sure how her longtime dream of building a family would happen anyway. Savannah looked at her watch, it read 10:30 pm. She handed the bartender a twenty to pay for the drinks. Then she reached into her leather purse for her phone. She noticed two missed calls from Greg. She made a mental note to call him back once she got in the car. She ordered her car which was three minutes away. She grabbed her belongings, and walked outside to wait for her ride.

The night was warm with a full moon gazing over the big city. Surprisingly, she could still see the stars in the sky, despite all the city lights. Savannah's phone began ringing just as her driver arrived. Greg was calling, she answered him as she got into the car.

"How are you, thanks so much for picking me up" she says to the driver. The driver said "Hey," as he glanced at Savannah in the rearview mirror, nodding. "Just wanted to be sure you had the correct address," Savannah questioned the driver. "The driver said, "I have 41st street, is that right?"

"Yes it is," Savannah confirmed as she relaxed in the back seat.

Answering the call Savannah says, "Hey, I was just about to call you back." Greg responds, "It's okay you're fine. Me and Jessie just been waiting for our favorite girl to come home. I was hoping you weren't working late again" Greg asks.

"No, I wasn't working late, I was out catching up with Lisa." Savannah says relaxing into the seat. Greg takes a deep breath and sighs on the phone.

"You forgot again, didn't you? You did this the last time Savannah. Jessie was cooking dinner for us tonight to celebrate her new book release," Gregs said. His frustration can be heard and felt. "Damn," Savannah says uncomfortably. "I thought it was tomorrow night. Please tell her how sorry I am to have missed this, so so so sorry. I'm on my way home now. I'll make it up to her in multiple ways tonight," says Savannah strongly.

"Hmmm…in multiple ways, huh?" Greg relaxes and responds aroused. "Yeah you better, I'm waiting right here by the dining room table!" Jessie says in the background.

"On my way y'all, I promise," Savannah said. Greg responds, "See you when you get here." They both say bye and end the call.

Twenty minutes later, Savannah finally arrives home, she walks in the door with her purse and white leather business tote bag and places it on the ground by the door. She places her keys on the wooden table where a nice portrait sits of Greg, Jessie, and Savannah holding hands and smiling on a beach. This photo of them always reminds her of happiness and home sweet home. Savannah walks to the kitchen and sees Greg looking in the fridge. Greg turns around and notices Savannah's presence in the kitchen.

"I'm home my loves." Savannah says warmly. Greg comes over to kiss her on the lips and hugs her. "Glad you home baby, finally," Greg said.

Savannah walks over to as she Jessie grabs a plate from the cabinet and passes it to Savannah while also kissing her on the lips. Jessie with her short but muscular frame, grabs a huge pot of crab casserole and carries it to the dining room table.

"I'm glad our queen is finally home too, now let's get to the juicy part and start eating. I've been craving this all night. I gotta tell you all about the book release party," Jessie said as she walked back to the kitchen.

Greg grabs them both by the waist, kisses their forehead, and walks them to the dining room table. Greg says "We're excited. We want to hear all about it, Jess." The three of them sat at the table. The group talked, enjoying the casserole and drinks as each recounted their respective day. By midnight, Greg was washing dishes, Jessie was on the couch drinking a beer and watching a football game, and Savannah retired to the bedroom where she sat in bed with her laptop working on a presentation. By 1 am, Jessie and Greg joined Savannah in their king-size bed. Upon seeing her loves enter the room, Savannah took the que, putting away her laptop and taking her place in bed. The three of them slept comfortably cuddled up together under the covers.

***

"Girl, where is our food? We've been sitting here for almost 30 minutes." Lisa said to Savannah sitting in the restaurant.

This particular restaurant was known for catering to diverse people of all backgrounds and identities. A small restaurant owned by an older gay couple. The place was always busy during the week and more so on the weekends. Patrons often remarked about the large rainbow flag prominently displayed on the company's front window. Though small, the eatery had an upscale style with marble tables and small rainbow flags embedded in the corners of their napkins.

"Be patient Lisa. I'm sure it'll be out soon", Savannah said. Her tone pleaded for Lisa to calm down. "You sound a little tense, I thought you'd be floating on clouds after last night's fun episode," Savannah continued sipping her latte.

"Tuh, I thought so too, but nothing happened! All she wanted to do was talk and talk some more. She wanted to and I quote 'Get to know each other better first and move slow.' Savannah, I ain't tryna get back into another relationship right now. Not after the devastation with Brittany." Lisa says as she looks at Savannah in frustration.

"I know, I know. Sorry you didn't have a wild fun night like you expected. Well, look on the bright side at least you are getting out there and meeting new people. Eventually, you will screw somebody soon!" Savannah said reassuring Lisa.

"Damn right. I need sex. At least some cuddling action. I'm grabbing any woman that says hi to me today," Lisa joked.

"Okay, we only got an hour for our lunch so we need all the time to eat. Like what's the hold up here today?" Lisa says as she scans the restaurant for their waiter. "Here's a candy bar, eat this, because we got a bigger problem to face here," says Savannah tossing the candy to Lisa. "Let that hold you over 'till the food comes." Savanna continues.

"Like what? The neglect I feel from the waitress due to my extreme HUNGER? What is this restaurant doing to me" said Lisa jokingly.

"I haven't finished our presentation for the board meeting next week. I've been working on it for weeks now and still haven't gotten it completed. Plus Dr. Tina has been hounding me with emails asking for the updates." Savannah said nervously.

"Chile you'll get it done like you always do. Girl, I don't know why you're stressing. Don't let all these work obligations get under your skin so much. You have been doing amazing work for years now." Lisa says reassuring her friend.

"Thank you girl, but you're not the one who has to deliver this presentation. And in front of the CEO herself! This is a huge deal!" Savannah said. Lisa responded with an eye roll.. "Savannah, just relax, you got this. If you need help, I can ask one of our volunteers or interns to do the video portion of the presentation. I'm sure they would love to help. Besides Justin, the intern, has been asking to do more work around the office anyway. I'll throw it to him."

Savannah contemplates, "Umm. Well…I feel Justin is one of those judgy gay types who's always in the church.. He probably doesn't want to work on an advertisement for colorful flavor condoms," Savannah laughs.. I'll just give him the Youth LGBT Visibility on Campus project that's needed for next month, he might like that better."

"Girl bye!" Lisa exclaims. "His little ass needs to be involved in any safer sex campaigns we have at the office. He's probably kissing all the men at his school and fucking all the men in his church choir." Lisa and Savannah houl in laughter. "He would be *the* perfect person for this. Send me the details and I'll add it to his list of tasks. He can add it to his internship credit." Lisa said, laughing but serious.

"Girl, you a mess and wrong talkin' about him like that. But if you think he'll be good, go ahead and run it by him. I need all the help I can get right now cause Dr. Tina is going to fire me if I mess this up for The LGBTQ+ Justice Collective." Savannah said.

"Just relax, you'll do fine." Lisa said reaffirming Savannah's long history of positive work ethic.

"Oh look, our food has finally arrived after such a long exhausting wait." Lisa says dramatically, tossing a fake smile at the waitress. The waiter places the food on the table with silverware and extra napkins. "Oh sorry about that wait. It's so busy here during lunchtime on Fridays. Can I get you something else to drink or another entree to go?" asked the waitress

"I'm fine ma'am. Can you bring me a to-go box and the checks? The checks are separate." Savannah said.

"Yes ma'am I'll be back shortly." the waitress said smiling. Just as the waitress walked away, Davis walked in wearing his plumbing uniform. He took a seat at the table with the girls.

Davis greets the ladies and sits down. "Hey, ladies! I think I may need your help with something."

Lisa responds, "It depends, ain't no telling what your crazy butt might need!" .

Davis looks at Lisa and smiles hard in agreement.

"How do you tell a woman delicately she needs to buy edge control for her rough edges? Cause y'all need to inform your waitress who just left the table." David says jokingly. They all laugh at Davis's remark. "Boy you crazy as hell! We can't take you nowhere." Lisa says laughing.

Savannah grabs a napkin and says "Anyway, instead of joking about innocent people and their edges, tell me how have you've been?"

"I been okay I guess. Just busy working. Tryna get all the installments in and out the way." Davis says, leaning back in his chair. Savannah looks out the window at the rainbow flag waving in the breeze.

"Well, we miss you, Mr. Hardworking man. I gotta admit though, I'm surprised you joined us at this restaurant," Savannah said with a twinge of astonishment in her voice.

"What do you mean surprised? Um, Savannah although I'm a masculine gay man I still have a stomach. A man gotta eat regardless of how flamboyant this place looks."says convincingly.

"I'm just saying 'cause the place has gay-friendly logos and stickers everywhere. I would hate for your homeboys at the barbershop and mechanic shop to walk by the window and see you eating here. And expose your DL cover secret." Savannah said as she and Lisa laughed.

"Ha Ha ha. Very funny, I told y'all a million times I'm not down low or in the closet. I'm just a discreet man who wants his privacy. No shame in that. I'm a proud Black gay man who doesn't have to walk around expressing it to everybody. Besides, the fellas already know. It just never came up yet." Davis said becoming a little annoyed by that tired joke the girls have been throwing at him for years.

Lisa looks at Savannah and they notice Davis getting a little uncomfortable, they rolled their eyes and decided to change the subject. Since college, Davis never publicly announced or cared to express his sexuality to anyone besides them. They also wondered how he navigated through life like this for so long having a major part of himself shielded from the world. Davis was masculine presenting with a tall muscle build and broad shoulders, he could easily pass for straight and no one would question.

Over the years, its seems that Davis was comfortable with letting folks think just that. The two ladies never imposed on his choice of privacy because they knew he had a right to his own self expression and identity. He had his own philosophy and definition of being "a proud Black gay man." They just decided years ago to simply be supportive and be patient with him in his journey, and when he wanted to express his truth to the public, they would be right there to have his back no matter the reactions of family and friends. Davis needed a true safe space to vent and be his authentic self, and Savannah and Lisa knew that special place was here with them. They were his diary, his rock, and his refuge and he'd been their strong brother they could always turn to for support.

"Well, whatever Davis. We hear ya and understand," said Savannah smiling at Lisa.

"By the way, how did the book signing go with Jessie last night? I wanted to go but I was stuck installing a sink in one of my clients' kitchen." Davis asked.

"Well y'all, I forgot again." Savannah said disappointed. "Wait, again! Savannah you have to stop forgetting about things like that. That's a major achievement for your girlfriend." Lisa said surprised by her friend's lack of consideration.

Lisa continued "If I knew she had a book release party we could have rescheduled our girls' night."

"I know, I know, you guys. I already feel terrible about it. I've been stressed over this huge presentation . It's taking over my whole life, it seems." Savannah whined.

"I think you, Greg, and Jessie need another vacation together. It's been a while anyway. You most definitely need a break Savannah!" Davis said.

"Chile I agree with Davis, a break and passionate romantic night with Greg and Jessie somewhere exotic is exactly what you need because you have been on work overload and that's not healthy, Van," Lisa says expressing concern for Savannah's wellbeing and mental health.

"Well, a vacation does sound good right now. I know I need one." Savannah says contemplating and milling over details in her mind.

"Yep think about it, hard girl. You should get away. But what did Jessie say about you not showing up… AGAIN?" Lisa asked, taking a bite of her food.

"I don't really know. I think Jessie is kinda mad at me, but she didn't say anything about it. We just talked about our day and went to sleep like normal. But I am determined to get my life organized. I need a home calendar so I can keep track of anything around me. That's my goal." Savannah said with resolve. "I don't know how you've been keeping up anyway. I'm surprised y'all three are still together after all these years. I don't know how you bisexual couples, or open relationship types, or poly-experimental types, or whatever you call it work. That's too many emotions, different personalities mixing, and important dates to remember in my life. Hell, I would barely remember my work tools if it weren't for my tool belt. But having to love two people every day and keep an equal balance. Naw, I can't," Davis said, leaning back in his chair and drinking a beer.

"What we three share is special. We always manage to make it work. They are my soulmates and source of happiness. As a bisexual woman, I get the best of both worlds with Greg and Jessie. I just need to purchase a large planner and calendar. I'm aiming to get my shit together this year. I got this covered," Savannah said.

"Now, that's the right attitude girl, spoken like the ambitious and determined woman I've always known.

We need to get back to the office because Dr. Tina is leading the meeting for the staff today. Which is in a couple of minutes." Lisa said.

"Well ladies y'all enjoy your day, meanwhile I'm going to order some appetizers." Davis said as both women got up from the table. Lisa quickly remembered some things to ask Davis she had previously forgotten.

"Oh yeah, Davis, when are you going to register to volunteer for the 'Stop The Discrimination' campaign for the downtown protest? Dr. Tina has been asking about you since the last creative meeting." Savannah continued.

"Hmm, I think Dr. Tina might have a thing for you Davis," Savannah says thoughtfully. Davis looked up at Savannah, shocked at her shocking remark.

"But I don't date women though and I'm still amazed how women have crushes on me and find me attractive," says Davis with confusion and slight humor.

"I mean you still are a man and remember people out here still think you're stra- I mean attractive. It's not like you're feminine or running around with a rainbow shirt on. You should be flattered because me and Lisa are disgusted by the sight of you." Savannah laughs.

Davis smirks and squints his eyes at her for the comment. They always found a way to tease and joke with one another. Every time they met they continued this banter and rousing, it was almost like a fun routine they all shared. It was their shared humor and stories together that solidified their friendship.

"Oh, whatever, but yeah I'll come. The rally is scheduled for 2 weeks from now right:" asked Davis to Lisa.

"Yep! So I'll put you on the volunteer roster and mail you a reminder a few days before." Lisa confirmed.

"Wait, before you go, what's the name of the new sexy man in the office? I saw him last time, you know the one who wore the tight blue shirt with pink shorts" Davis said, biting his lip. "Girl, I think he's talking about Justin the intern. He's the only one I can think of with that style. But um, that one right there is like a dog in heat. Plus Justin is only 22. You don't want those young college boy problems, Davis." Lisa said as she walked towards the door, erasing the thought for Davis. However, Davis made a mental note to bring this up again in the near future.

***

The two women got in the car and drove back to the office. They both walked into the building to hear their Executive Director Dr. Tina already giving her speech to the staff. They quietly found two empty seats at the back of the wooden conference table by a window. They relaxed themselves in their chairs and listen as the address precedes.

Dr. Tina stood before the staff and gave the following address:

"I'm proud to say we have been in service for 10 years to our LGBTQ+ community here at the LGBTQ Justice Collective. As a Black transwoman growing up in the South, I always dreamed of a time when I would have a team of people around me to aid me in fighting for legal protection, mobilization of a movement, and creating paths to liberation for all identities of queerness, gender, and people of color. I had to overcome so much in my journey including racism, transphobia, verbal abuse, and even sexual violence.. I stand before you today not only as a survivor but as a source of strength and determination, leading the charge and continuing the call to action. After graduating from law school, I knew my life as a Black transwoman would be an act of marvelousness and also an act of beautiful rebellion. I was born to do a mission just like many of you here before me. We must continue to dismantle systemic oppression, educate our society, and lead by example. We must show the world how to love and show compassion as humans. Humanity needs this like we need air and water. I am so enthusiastic about launching our projects for the year. The 'STOP Discrimination Campaign', the 'Youth LGBTQ Visibility on Campus Project', 'End AIDS Now', and our new ad "Safer Sex is Delicious" which will air on several broadcast and digital channels as early as next week, thanks to our very own Communications and Media manager Savannah Jones. I am so thrilled and honored to wake up every day to come to an office of brilliant leaders, innovative thinkers, and proactive activists like yourselves, no like really though y'all, this organization is here because of all of y'all great work. Pat yourselves on the back, but not too long! We still have more work to do and more change to make in this world. So, with all that being said we've got another great year ahead of us in social justice work. I need everyone in each department to email me your position in each of our projects this year as clarity of your duties. The office deadline has been moved up to next Wednesday, another 5 days. So everyone enjoy your weekend. I need to see emails in my inbox and folders on my desk by next Wednesday. No exceptions. Have a great weekend, the meeting is adjourned."

Lisa and Savannah both rose from their chairs, along with other staff members and headed to their respective offices. When Savannah reached her desk she immediately started checking her emails and went to work on her presentation. The office was beginning to quiet down from the normal after-meeting chatter. She heard a vibration from her purse where the phone was stored. She reached down to grab the phone and noticed it was a text message from Jessie. It read "Can we talk? I need to get something off my chest." Savannah saw the message and instantly froze.

Women of My Kind

Women of my kind
Women of my kind
Women of my kind
We are so divine.

Women of my kind
Have hair that can be
Afros
Straight
Curly
Braids
Locs
That ought to be celebrated in every room

Women of my kind
Have noses that are
Full
Wide
Round
Small
Slender

Of the color brown, black, and other glorious
hues

Women of my kind
Have experienced
Days
Nights
Months
Seasons
Of the sweetest and saddest of human emotions

Women of my kind
Have often felt
The highest of pleasure and deepest of intimacy
at night
Yet, the deafest of silence and swiftest
abandonment in the morning

Women of my kind
Are too familiar with
Loving, supporting, and celebrating with sisters
and brothers today
Just to hear their eulogies and witness their
vigils tomorrow

Women of my kind

Have always known
We have been right there on the frontlines and
in the center of activism movements
Yet, the streets and mainstream media keep us
hidden like pariahs

Women of my kind
Harness abilities that are
Metamorphosis
Herbal medicine
Sexual healing
Aura and Energy transcending
Women of my kind
Come in different versions that can be
Tall or petite
Slim or thick
Penis or vagina
Only Hormones or all Surgery
Just know when you see us, we are unique,
ancient, and royalty.

So, when you see me
You see her
You see us
The Royal Concubine Women
The Mermaid Women
The Transgender Women
The Lost Atlantan Women
The Amazonian Women
The African and Indigenous Priestess Women

These are all my sisters
Women of Mysticism and Mystery
Women of my kin and soul ties

Women of my kind
Women of my kind
Women of my kind
We are so divine.

Treasures of the Matriarch

A Black Queer Romance Fantasy

Her feet slid through the soft sand as she sat on the beach getting her hair braided by Mushu. The two women noticed a boat in the distance cruising towards them in the sparkling blue sea. The wind was blowing but not hard enough to cause a cool breeze. Aya periodically dipped her toes in the nearby shallow water to get a cool sensation to rush through her body.

"Looks like a man and a young child, but can't make it out yet" Aya said, squinting her eyes to see in the bright sun.

"It's probably just them Tulsa boys coming to visit her again. It is nice to see them make that trip for her like that as she heals."

"You think she's gonna be okay? Aya asked, hoping Mushu could give her some solace about her neighbor's health.

"Only the moon knows if she's gonna heal or if these are her last days to return home. And all we can do is support her and be there for her." Mushu said wisely.

Aya understood but took a deep sigh knowing it's all in the moon's hands. Mushu notices as Aya slips into deep thought that gives her an air of hopelessness.

"Oop, it's done. Go look at your braids. Girl, I think I did it with the pattern this time. Go look! You look good!". Mushu motions to Aya to embrace her hair in the hand mirror.

"Yes! You did it. It's beautiful Mu. Thanks girl. This pattern ...yeah I really like it. Only one thing is missing though, them cute gold braid clips you got. Can you put some in my hair?" Aya asks, thinking of a clever beauty tip.

"Oh yeah, that would look good with it. I'll put them on when we get back to the temple."Mushu says planning.

The boat was now near the coastline preparing to dock not too far from the two women sitting on the beach. They could see a dark skinned man with a long haired child stepping off the boat, placing their feet on the warm sand. The boat had boxes of clothes and items. The child looked no older than 10 or 12 years old, they figured. They couldn't tell if the child was happy or sad to be here from their long voyage but they started to realize this wasn't the Tulsa boys visiting, this was a man dropping off his child to leave on the island. The man and the child started to unload their boxes and walk toward the largest building on the island, The Temple of Iza.

The women knew this could only mean one thing, whenever one of the male outsiders took a child to that building...an orphanage. Everybody knew across the many islands that the building wasn't only for orphans, but also the homeless, poor, throwaways, and the feminine Javoras.

And yes, as the women looked closer, the child was a Javora, a person that was a boy-girl or girl-boy. A person that is clearly a mixture of feminine and masculine energy, or androgynous. The child definitely couldn't stay on the island of men. It was tradition to send all feminine Javoras to our island of women. Which meant the highest honor to the Great Mother of the Island, Mother LaRa. Rumor has it that they are her favorite kind of people and children. She always does a Moon Welcoming Ceremony for new women entering the island, but she seems to always have a sense of deep joy and happiness about herself for new feminine Javoras. So,Mushu and Aya were too ready to bring the news to Great Mother LaRa. This also meant Mushu and Aya would now have a new little friend to mentor and show the ropes to. This was exciting.

Mushu greets the two visitors with a quick wave, then heads inside the temple to go into her room. Leaving Aya to do her usual hospitality duties as a royal greeting the guests formally.

Aya walks up to the visitors and notices the man talking to the child.

"Listen, you are about to meet the lady that runs this place. Smile and say thank you if she gives you anything. Be on your best behavior, ya hear me. It's gonna be okay. This island got people just like you that's umm...different. You'll make friends easily here" the man said to the child.

Aya overheard the instructions and walked closer to the two as the speech ended.. Aya greeted the child.

"Hey beautiful! I'm glad you made it here. I'm Aya, daughter of Mother LaRa.

What's your name?" Aya asks the child warmly while the man smiles watching Aya.

"Um hey, I'm Lamar, um but I...my nickname is Layla. I prefer that..." Layla says a little nervous and stuttering.

"Then around here baby, your name is Layla. Welcome to your new home," Aya says to Layla, giving her a warm hug. The man speaks again, almost interrupting.

"Hey Princess Aya, I don't mean to be rude, do I leave him with you or with your mother? My bad, I mean do I leave her! I'm trying my best with this new pronoun thing. But yeah. I got to head back soon." The man says a little awkwardly.

"You not staying for the Moon Welcome Ceremony? Most parents stick around for that at least and make sure their child gets settled. Plus, do you have your brass bowl of freshwater or flowers to give to Mother LaRa? That's also our tradition to give Mother LaRa her favorite gifts as a newcomer." Aya said sternly.

Um, yes the flowers are in one of these boxes. That's for her. I could stay awhile longer, maybe a day or two. By the way, I'm the older brother, he's not my son. I mean daughter." the man says to Aya, still smiling.

Aya notices the man's dark ebony muscular arms as he held the box. Looking to his face she saw the dimples in his jawline. She sensed something from him but tries to ignore it. He hands her gold flowers inside a brass vase.

"Well...look at this, I think she'll love it. I'll take you both to her. I'm sure she's in the main room. Follow me." Aya says, leading them inside the temple.

"Oh I like your hair. Nice style," the man says to Aya.

"Thank you. I didn't get your name," Aya asked him while guiding Layla by the hand as they proceeded through the hallway.

"I'm Davalii, farmer and merchant of the North Islands of Cape Verde. I sell vegetables, spices, and herbs. I'm doing very well, I must

say. Plus. I'm quite good with my hands too."
Davalii says to Aya with charm and flirtation.

Aya can truly sense the man being
charming, and she continues to ignore his
advances.

"Ok, Davalii, your name sounds
Senegalese to me. Am I right ? Aya asks to
change the direction of the conversation,

"Not quite, I'm from an island town
called Santa Maria of Cape Verde, not too far
from here. But my parents do have lots of
friends in Senegal so I traveled back and forth
as a kid there. But because you said it, I'll take
it." Davalii says with a charming smile.

The three of them finally reach the main
room where the Great Mother LaRa was
pouring water and tending to her home garden.
She adorns a long gold dress, a cowrie shells
necklace and brass bracelets. Mother LaRa was
also sporting her luscious afro which resembles
a crown framing her oval brown face.

"Ma, we have a visitor *AND*, a beautiful
newcomer to the island," says Aya .

"Thanks baby." Great Mother LaRa says to her daughter, as she stops her child for a warm embrace. Great Mother LaRa then turns to speak to the newcomers.

"Welcome to the Island of Iza! Make yourselves comfortable. I see you two came a day early. I figured that might have been you two, when I saw the boat through my Temple window". Mother LaRa said hugging them as well.

"A day early? Wait Ma, you knew they were coming?" Aya asked in surprise.

"Honey, I'm the highest matriarch of these islands. I see and hear all things. Remember that. But yes, their parents spoke with me weeks ago about our darling Layla." Great Mother LaRa said as she smiled and winked at Layla.

"But I hadn't set up a room for her in the temple yet. Well... let me go clean up for you Layla. I'll get your bed ready first. Give me a few minutes, I'll be back." Aya said hurrying off.

"Daughter, relax. It's handle. I did the room myself." Great Mother LaRa said stopping Aya in her tracks.

Aya was taken aback by the idea of her mother cleaning up a room. With all the maids, tasks, and businesses she governs. But then she remembers the rumors about her own mother from the early days.

"You haven't cleaned a room since our last..." Aya says then gets interrupted swiftly.

"Girl, be quiet and mind your business. Help this young man to his room. I believe you're staying only til after the ceremony, correct?" Mother LaRa says with both sternness and grace.

"Um, Yes ma'am. I have to tend to some business back at home on the men's island then sailing again to Sierra Leone for vegetable deliveries. But I definitely will be at the ceremony and I have my gift for you here." says Davalii with assurance.

"Okay, then. A young man that respects Mother Earth and travels providing food and greenery across the Ivory Coast. Okay, young man, I'm impressed. Keep it up. So many other young folks are leaving farming and agriculture for that technology world. It's good to see a young man still caring about and connected to our ecosystem.

Mother LaRa takes the flower gift with one hand and motions Layla to walk with her to the garden.

"You wanna learn more about the mystical flowers in my garden? They can grant me wishes and create medicine! Mother LaRa says in a joyful and playful manner like a schoolteacher to Layla.

"Yes ma'am!" Layla says anxious and excited.

Aya and Davalii look back at the two giggling and pointing at the different flowers. Aya hasn't seen her mama this happy in awhile. Children always had a special place in her mother's heart.

Especially the young Javoras. Aya takes Davalii to his temporary room he will occupy during his visit and

allows him some space to get settled. Aya walks to her room, where she sees Mushu knocked out sleeping in the chair with a book in her hand. Mushu has a habit of reading and falling asleep on Aya's bedroom couch, then leaving in the middle of the night to retire to her own room. Aya shakes her head and lays in bed to rest. She makes a mental note to remind Mushu to help her with the gold hair clips. A perfect look for the Moon Welcoming Ceremony.

* * *

The next morning, upon waking up
Aya's eyes landed on the painting of the
beautiful Yoruba Orisha Logun Ede. For years
this wall painting has been the first thing Aya
sees each morning but today she noticed that the
androgynous deity gave her serenity and joy.
Orisha Logun Ede was a beautiful divine being,
adorned in their colorful peacock feathers.

She can also hear sounds of the ocean
waves and men talking outside her temple walls.
The sound of many African men's voices, with
different dialects and accents of their native
tongue from the surrounding islands.

Living on an Island of only women, the
sounds of men's voices felt both foreign and
soothing at the same time. Which was very
refreshing.

She could see the blue ocean waves
dancing outside her window and the dozens of
boats with men from all shades of brown and
black hues of toffee to deep mocha. Each man
was dressed in clothing in honor of Earth Day. It
was the island tradition and culture to have
Earth Day once a month where the local island

residents come together to help clean the shores. The men took the time to visit the women's island to help with yard labor, heavy lifting, home repairs, and more. But of course, this also meant the mingling of all genders socializing with each other. This typically leads to flirting and side conversations while working to help clean Mother Earth. This was most definitely a human's version of a mating season and community service day all mixed together.

As Aya gets dressed for the day in comfy green tube dress as she checks her hair she hears Mushu's footsteps walking towards her room. Mushu enters the room in a simplistic green tank top and White jean shorts. She has a green flower in her hair giving her a look of calm paradise.

"Good morning girl. You got any shea or cocoa butter? I need to put some on these ashy legs."Mushu says.

"Yeah, it's in the top draw over there." Aya says pointing towards her vanity mirror dresser.

"I guess the day started because all I hear is men outside. But somebody already got

her a man so none of them even matter, huh?"
Mushu says teasing while Aya lotions her legs.

"Girl who? What you mean?" Aya says
as she puts on her gold earrings.

"Who, who, who, said the owl. Girl you!
I wasn't even in the room and I felt the vibes
that Davalii was giving you." Mushu says
continuing to tease Aya who is now smiling and
blushing.

"Girl bye, I ain't thinking about him.
Besides, he's a man that travels a lot for work.
That sounds like a long distance relationship to
me and I don't need that in my life." Aya said,
irritated at the thought of it.

"Okay! You said something then Ya. I
can't even argue there. I mean living on a
fucking island with other women is cute but we
need a male visitor to deliver us a big package
on the daily! Not a man that's always distant
and never home." said Mushu with certainty.

The two women laugh and high five
each other in agreement.

"He's handsome though, no lie. But I really don't know, girl. It's still all new anyway. Plus he may not even be into women like me. You know... all of me". Aya says in reflection.

"Yeah you're right. Well, you know what I always say about that. You are a diamond, he better

smell the palm trees and get with it. The javora girls are infinite, magical, and beautiful, right?

It's gonna be his loss if he doesn't care to love all of you Ya. You are beautiful just the way you are. Not to mention girl, you are basically a real princess of this island. Never forget that."

Mushu says, in hopes of restoring Aya's confidence.

It was always nice to have a friend like Mushu to be there to remind Aya that no matter the type of woman she was, she was valuable, beautiful, and worthy! Mushu was a true sister. Aya and Mushu had been friends since they were kids. Each could not imagine life without the other. Aya might be royalty here on the island, but she didn't feel that way in a large world that tries to erase a Javoras' existence. She often heard horror stories about how women and girls like her were treated in other parts of the world. But, no matter what the other people of the world might say or think of her style of woman, on this island at least, all types of women are regarded as sacred beings.

The island has always been a safe haven and refuge for javoras ever since its origin, 400 hundred years ago when a Polynesian King married a Javora woman of South Africa, Aya's great great great grandmother. The King knew there weren't many places she could travel to, especially due to the European rise of colonization that was happening at the time. Casting out people in tribes that didn't fit into their Chrisitan community and values. Upon marriage, he purchased and gifted her one of the islands of Cape Verde as a new home and safe place for all Javoras of Africa to live, visit, and even be dropped off when a tribe, village, or parent didn't want the colonizers to hurt or kill them. Their enterprise began a new tradition where tribes and villagers sent ships to take their Javoras to our Island of Iza. Through the King's wealth and her brilliant vision, they both managed to create a growing community with a schools, a hospital, a bank, and multiple stores. They even formed a military of warrior men from nearby islands for protection and support. But the trustest gem that was gained from the island is the first Javora Queen, the first Great Mother LaRa Aya's great great great grandmother who enjoyed walking on her island at night always claimed there were magical waters that watched over the island to render blessings, messages, and protection.

A bond was created between her and the magical waters where she was directed to host Moon Welcoming Ceremonies for newcomers to the island. Over the last two hundred years stories of the island's ceremonies and safe haven for Javoras and women refugees gained the attention of women far and wide. The island began to bring in an influx of women who fled persecution and patriarchal dictatorship, which caused an expansion of welcoming women of any nationality, languages, and all women refugees who wanted a better life and freedom to thrive. The island evolved into a matriarchal society, naturally, one of the few that still remains in the world today. Island of Iza.

"I know. Thanks girl. I be letting the world get to me sometimes, but I know I'm royalty. But anyway... let's head out. I need to head to the health center to pick up my hormones and Ms. Tulsa's medicine while I'm there. I'm sure Ma got some gardening work for me to do too." Aya said.

The two women leave the temple and walk towards the island's health center. While catching the eye of a few of the visiting men. Aya notices Davalii in the crowd of men who were working. She begins to power walk to the front door of the health center. Mushu realizes what Aya is doing and laughs.

* * *

Aya walks out of the health center with all her and Ms. Tulsa meds in a tote bag. As she walks with Mushu towards Ms. Tulsa house, an ocean breeze flows through her braids and cools her scalp, a sensation that never gets old. They reached the older woman's house, which had a wheelchair ramp for easy access for Ms. Tulsa. Mushu knocked on the door and waits, allowing time for Ms. Tulsa to hear and reach the front door. The older woman who was wearing a satin muumuu smiles brightly at the young women who came to visit.

"Aww, looka here, it's my favorite two girls again... welcome baby... come in. " the old woman says between coughs.

"Hey Ms. Tulsa we just wanted to give you your medicine and check on ya." Aya says taking out the meds and placing them on the counter.

"Thanks baby. Did you all want some to eat? I got some yams and cornbread on the stove, ya hear. Make yourselves comfortable." says Ms. Tulsa generously

"Um. Not today Ms. Tulsa thanks though. We weren't staying too long." Mushu says.

"Oh ok, well give your mama this blanket I finished making. I put a little gold in there just the way she likes it. Here baby." Ms. Tulsa said, handing her the blanket.

"Aww thanks Ms. Tulsa She's going to love this, it's really cute too." Aya says looking at the handmade blanket.

"You know what else is cute, them strong men outside working. I might be old but this woman still got...eyes. Hmmhm." Ms. Tulsa says witty and sharp.

"Wait! Yes Ms. Tulsa! I know that's right. Mushu says laughing and shaking her head.

Aya and Mushu sits down on the couch as Ms. Tulsa parks her wheelchair on the side of the couch. A few seconds of silence pass between them as the radio plays in the background.

The sound of the oldies, classic R&B music flowed from the speakers. Mushu notices an old photograph of Ms. Tulsa.

The photos is of Ms. Tulsa as a younger photo of herself as a little girl with older women all dressed in an office dress.

Mushu saw it many times but never got a chance to ask about it. She uses this moment as an opportunity to explore her curiosity.

"Ms. Tulsa, is that you in the picture on the wall?" Mushu asks in hopes to learn more.

"Oh yeah, that's little me standing with the ladies at the bank where my mama used to work at, way back in Tulsa, Oklahoma. Tuh, before them people destroyed everything us Blacks worked so damn hard to build.

Ugh, this photo is so bittersweet to me girls, but I keep it to remind me of a time where we owned and made major decisions for our own people." Ms. Tulsa looks down at the floor and takes a deep sigh. A memory and deep emotions arise up in her.

"I'm so sorry Ms. Tulsa, you and so many people, our people, had to experience that. I read about that in history books but it's nothing like living through it." Aya says, consoling Ms. Tulsa rubbing her shoulder.

"Yeah baby it makes me so angry that they try not to even mention our contributions and let alone a whole enterprise Black folks made on our own. Our own fucking town and they ripped it from us burned and destroyed our community. You know so many families were broken, and displaced, all I remember as a little black girl was the fear of surviving. Them white folks wasn't gonna just let me go to school and live free next to them. I jus, just...."

Aya leaned over more to hold her hand and Ms. Tulsa took a moment to breathe and regain herself after having a flashback of her childhood. A reminder of all she lost. She lost her home, her future, her agency, and the many many people she was mourning. A few seconds of silence came.

And Mushu thought to ask a question to bring lightness to the depth of sadness that appeared in the room.

"Is that where you got your name?"

"Yep. That's what the folks called me when I arrived here. It has stayed ever since. I remember fleeing, pissed off like so many other Black families. There was nowhere else in America that felt like true sovereignty and freedom we had as Black people. Some folks stayed in America, others like me migrated away. Some went to the Caribbeans, some to Canada. But when I was old enough I heard of this island of women near Africa, mostly with Black and African women. Oh I saved up my

money and ran to get the nearest flight to
Senegal, then sailed here in a large ferry. I
remember the smell and feel of the island back
then, the scent of ocean water and sand. You
know that's how I met your Grandma, way back
then. Such a sweet woman. "Ms. Tulsa says in
reflection.

"Oh wow! You met my grandma, Ms.
Tulsa? Aya asked in disbelief and happiness.

"Oh yeah, such a strong and tall woman
too, but nobody messed with her. Your grandma
was a sweet woman, a true protector of us on
this island. A firecracker! Oh yes mhmm."
Ms.Tusla said with a hard laugh, as an old
memory passes her mind.

Aya took in this moment staring at the
photo and wondering about the other survivors
of the Tulsa Massacre. What were their stories
and deep feelings? Aya also thought about who
her grandma was amongst other women during
her prime. A moment of silence came again,
then Aya remembered to help Ms. Tulsa with
her medicine or house task.

"Ms.Tulsa, did one of your boys come by this week to see you? Do you need me to grab anything else?" Aya asked.

"Oh yea Johnny came by the day before to get me some groceries and the mail. I got everything I need, baby. Thanks suga." Ms. Tulsa says.

"That's good. And your meds? Did you get a chance to take them yet? Aya asks.

"Nah, I need to though. The doctor is on my ass about taking them pills. Hand me them pills off the counter over there." Ms. Tulsa says pointing at the counter with all her meds lined up.

Mushu walks towards the rest of Ms.Tulsa medicine and the new meds from the health center. Aya grabs a glass of water and helps Ms. Tulsa with each pill.

Taking her time to ensure all meds were taken and if she needed assistance with anything else.

Aya and Mushu stay for a little while longer catching up on a few things that they discussed on their last visit. A few minutes passes by and Aya and Mushu hugged Ms. Tulsa before heading out the door.

Ms. Tulsa stopped Aya before she closed the door and gives her a quick word before leaving.

"I see that young man might be into you young gal. Remember life is too short and there is more to this life than just a career, friends, and going to parties. A woman deserves good love too. Remember that okay. I was young once. And listen baby, yes you might be a different type of young lady, but love is still yours to claim." Ms. Tulsa said to Aya in a wise tone of voice.

"Yes ma'am I understand. I do deserve love too." Aya says in a serene knowing and gratitude for Ms.Tulsa wisdom in her life.

Out of nowhere Mushu yells from outside the house.

"See, I be tryna tell her Ms. Tulsa but she never listens to me!" Mushu says from outside.

All three women laugh, that deep belly laugh from the core.

* * *

Later that afternoon, the island had dozens of people moving around in small groups, all pitching in to clean the landscape. A group of people were picking up trash around the water, another group was working in the main garden collecting vegetables and

One group replanted seeds, another group was tending to the broken branches and wood, and a few folks were also on freshwater duty, simply walking around handing out water to folks and making sure everyone was okay and not overheating in the bright sun.

It became a community web of unity and connectivity to restore Mother Earth together. After hours of everyone working on different parts of the island and surrounding islands, a sense of both tiredness and accomplishment could be felt.

Folks begin to rest and huddle in groups around shade areas, talking amongst themselves.

While Mushu decided to be on water supply duty this time around, Aya was helping her mother in the garden. Many of the children were in the gardening group as well, all learning about sunlight, seeds, names of different flowers and vegetables. Layla was in this group of girls placing seeds in the soil and watching the many butterflies that were fluttering around. Aya could see in the distance, Davalli kneeling down talking and helping Layla and the other girls.

She smiles and for some reason enjoys this sweet moment of them gardening together. She must have been staring too long, because Davalii turned slightly to wave at her showing his pearly white teeth. His smooth dark skin was soaked in sweat from today's labor, but his energy still remained vibrant. Meanwhile, Aya was ready for a seat and a long bath. Davalli stood up and then rubbed his hands together, removing most of the soil. Then he started walking towards Aya. But of course Great Mother LaRa wasn't too far. She was close enough to eavesdrop on their conversation. As she tended to the garden under a shaded area.

"Hey Aya, how are you doing over here on the pile of soil? You need help or some tools? Davalii said looking at her with drops of sweat running down his muscular chest revealing years of outside labor.

I'm doing okay, I don't need any tools, maybe a break though. I've been at this for hours." Aya says.

"Well let's take a break. I can make us some water." Davali suggests before being interrupted by Great Mother LaRa.

"Ya'll should take a break over there on the bench. I made some Lemonade." Great Mother LaRa says interjecting and guiding them to talk more with each other. She was liking the idea of this young man with her daughter. But she still kept her discernment radar on him, just in case.

"Lemonade sounds amazing right now Mother LaRa, thank you!" Davalii said in agreement, thrilled with the suggestion.

Aya and Davalii walked to the bench area to rest and talk. Davalii poured the Lemonade in a glass for her as she sits down. They both get comfortable as they watch the many groups and cliques of people talking across the island.

"I guess it's social hour. Everybody is talking now, besides the kids." Davalii said, noticing his surroundings.

"Yeah, after all that work folks just want to chill, talk, and probably eat." Aya said.

"Yeah for sure. It's beautiful though how you all do this clean up and take care of the Earth. We need more of this throughout the west and the rest of the world. Y'all bring a new meaning to community service out here. Plus the brothers really respect the women around here.Like a real team. They even let them lead. We need more of that. I'm sorry. I'm probably just rambling on and on…um...How was your day?" Davalii asks.

"No, I like that you are observant and appreciate our customs and traditions. It's nice to hear from an outsider." Aya says.

"Woah, an outsider. Is this a secret club now?" Davalii says teasing her and cheesing hard.

"I don't mean it like that. You know like a person that is not from here." Aya says, clearing up and laughing.

"Yeah, I know what you mean. But this is your real hometown though. Like you and your family have been here for decades right? I suppose since you like a royal right? Davalii asks still trying to understand some of the island's history.

"Not like a royal. I'm actually a royal. We just don't rule and dictate our land like how they do in England or other countries. We are a matriarchal society. A village of women that believe we all are sacred feminine beings and our world centers the elder women and feminine wisdom. Life begins from a woman and so should societal functions. But just like you, I can ramble on and on about this. But yes to answer your question, this is my home and my people have been here for centuries actually. Aya says teaching him some of their traditions and customs.

"That's beautiful Aya, I mean Princess Aya. Miss Majesty. I really think your traditions are special. It might lead to a better world if more women led and made decisions like this. Real world peace even. I'm down. But one question, have you ever left the island?" Davalii asks.

"Oh I like how you say my title. It sounds more fancy. But yeah, I traveled around Africa a few times, never really explored much outside this region." Aya says in reflection.

"You gotta let me show you around! There is so much to see out there. Like the Himalayan mountains in Asia, the Americans with their football and Statue of Liberty, the Eiffel Tower in Paris, the Austrialians got this animal called a Kangaroo that hops, and so much more. Like it's really a big world." Davalli says with enthusiasm.

"Yeah I read and heard about all that already. Just never saw it in person. Not yet at least. Aya said with certainty.

"That's my point. You deserve to see and experience all that. We gotta go." Davalli said.

"Okay I guess, but they may not like or approve of women like me. Aya says quickly without thinking.

"What you mean?" Davalli asks, confused.

"Nothing." Aya says immediately.

"Huh?" Davalii says more confused than before.

"I mean like, you know, as a Matriarchal woman. They might not like my mindset." Aya said swiftly changing her answer from what she originally was thinking.

"Oh, there are plenty of feminist women in the west and all around now. I think you'll be fine." Davalii says, trying to reassure her.

"Well, feminism is slightly different from matriarchy, there are similarities but, we don't have to get into all that right now. But okay. Sounds like I might need to travel more." Aya says. She was relieved to have dodged that moment of disclosing too soon.

Time passes and their conversation flows. The two continued to talk for hours after the sunset and well into the night. Now and then getting up for food or a restroom break. But their chemistry and conversation remained vibrant. By the end of their long talk, Davalii walked Aya to the front door of the Temple, the two share a brief moment of staring into each other's eyes under the watchful moon. Davalii took a leap of faith and moved in with a warm hug and kiss. Her body allowed this romantic gesture, as she kisses back. They pull back slowly and smiled at each other, both looking joyful from unexpected intimacy.

"Good night Princess. I guess I'll See you tomorrow, right?

"Hmmm, let me check my schedule. Maybe."

They both laugh,

"Yeah, we got that big Moon Welcoming Ceremony tomorrow. So you will see me and everybody mama will too. I'm in it.

"Oh yeah for my lil sis Layla. I can't wait.

"Yeah it's magical, just know you will be in for a huge surprise!" Aya says with mystical certainty.

"Oh ok then. Well as long as I get a chance to talk to you, I'm going to have a great day.

"Hmmmm.... Really now. Ok then Davalii. Good night.

They hug again and Aya smiles as she walks into the temple to her room. Davaliii after a while goes to his guest room too. As most people slept, the night gave way to calm sounds of frogs, crickets, and ocean waves.

***

The next morning, Aya walks outside to the store and sees Mushu on the beach getting her own hair braided by Richie. Aya is always happy to see him visit the island with his beautiful spirit and warm energy. Not to mention, so many of the girls love him and his partner Leo. Richie does many of the girls' hair from time to time and Leo is an amazing artist, the best photographer and painter many have ever seen. Leo just has a great eye for capturing emotion and color schemes in his muses. Aya walks towards them in the tan sand, while they both wave to Aya on her way.

"Hey girl hey! You're looking good as always sis. What's the tea? - Richie says smiling as his latte colored skin glistens in the sun.

"Heeeey! Nothing much about to head to the store. Nah you looking good yourself. Oh, I love this purple highlight in your afro though. That's fly!" Aya says to Richie, who smiles and does a little dance to himself, not missing a beat on the hair braiding.

"You know me, I gotta spice it up sometimes. I say bring the colour!" Richie says with excitement.

"Ya, what store are you going to? Can you go grab..." Mushu asked.

'Girl not you giving me a shopping list already, ugh" Aya interjects jokingly. Richie and Aya laugh while Mushu sucks her teeth.

"Girl I got you. You want some snacks or something to drink?"

"Just a soda, gum, and some tampons. That's all. See, I wasn't even gonna work you like that. "Mushu says jokingly.

"Umhm...I got you though, girl. How's Leo doing? I haven't seen him over here in a while." Aya asks Richie.

"Chile cause he got that new corporate job now, a 9 to 5 working as a media consultant for this law firm." Richie says, braiding the last piece of Mushu's hair.

"Congratulations. That's good news. Wait, don't tell me he stopped doing his art? Aya asks.

"Nah, you know art is always gonna be his passion but he wants extra money and more stability. The art thing feeds his soul but the job actually can feed both of us, very nicely I might add." says Richie.

"Okay then, we are blessed and doing well, huh." Mushu says.

"Oh yes! Definitely. But Leo's ass will be around here next time he's off when y'all do free drinks at Club Lex again."

"Okay, and you know I'm down to go. You know that's every Thursday night." Mushu says.

"Yeah, I think he's gonna be off next Thursday, we 'll be back over here girl. Right in that new boat parked over there.." Richie says, pointing towards the water. They all glance over at the docking area where they see this black boat with a sparkling silver strip across the top, with leather cream seats.

"Okay fancyyyy!!! Oh you gotta take us on a ride." Aya says in pure excitement.

"Okay cool, you wanna ride now? I'm finished with Mu's hair actually." Richie ask.

Both women agree and they all walk through the shallow water where the boat is parked. They all get settled in, and right before they leave the shore, they see Davalii waving and running towards them.

"Girl there's a fine chocolate man waving and running over here. I know he aint for me. So which one of you ladies is he for?" Richie says turning off the boat's motor.

"That's Aya's new man. Chile the princess up and found herself a King," Mushu says, teasing Aya.

"Y'all hush. We just talking. But yeah he real cute." Aya says to them laughing.

Davalii finally makes it over to the boat.

"Hey Good morning everyone" Davalii says to greet everyone. They all speak in return.

"Hey are you about to leave? I wanted to take you out for breakfast. I hear it's this nice spot a few streets down. But I didn't want to pull you away from you friends like that. Just wanted to eat some food with you, talk, maybe explore the city before I leave in a few days." Davalii says in hopes she is interested.

"Girl you better go! Um... my name is Richie, nice to meet you, by the way." Richie says, sticking his hand out for a handshake. Davalli grins a little and shakes his hand.

"Nice to meet you man. Is it okay if I take this lovely lady out for breakfast?" Davalii asks Mushu and Richie.

"You can have her all week actually, she was getting on my last nerves anyway. " Mushu says quickly and teasing.

Davalii helps her climb out the boat and they wave bye to the two who slowly reverse the boat into the water. Davalii and Aya walk together passing different colored buildings until they reached the breakfast diner. The waiter sits them at a patio table with the view of the ocean. They talk and eat for a while, not skipping a beat. Their conversation flows smooth like yesterday.

After breakfast, they walked to the store and grabbed all the things Aya and Mushu needed for today.

But by the time they returned back to the temple it was afternoon and they were now sitting in the main living room watching TV. They talked amongst themselves as a few locals walked past them to the kitchen which has a public food pantry for the low-income community. After a few more minutes passed, the temple was silent and empty. Most people were out running errands before tonight's Moon Welcoming Ceremony. Aya takes a deep breath and decides maybe now is the right time to disclose and have a real talk with him.

Aya looks deeply into Davalii's eyes, and takes another deep breath.

"What's wrong?" Davalii asks with concern.

"So, I need to tell you something. I was waiting for the right time." Aya says with nervousness.

"Um ok. I'm listening. Is everything ok? Is this about Layla? Davalii asks.

"No Layla is fine, it's something else. About me. So listen, I'm a unique and different type of woman. And I'm not talking about just me being part of a royal family or raised in a matriarchal society. More than that. I'm like different… different." Aya says.

"Um ok? Different how? What are you talking about? Davalii ask with confusion and worry.

Different like…so… um…I'm a Javora! I wasn't ready or sure when to tell you, but yeah, I'm a javora. I probably should have said something last night when we..." Aya says nervously.

"Wait, is that what you worried about? I had a feeling since I landed on the island Aya. It's all good with me." Davalii says with relief and calm assurance.

"What! What do you mean you already know?" Aya says, shocked at his calm response.

"Nah, I didn't know, but let's be honest, this island is the only island in a 1,000 mile radius, maybe ever in history, to have a plethora of Javoras. I was more than prepared to run into a beautiful woman who just so happens to be a Javora. Aya it's literally like 80 percent of y'all right here on this island in the whole world." Davalii says matter of factly.

They both laugh. Davalii reaches to hold her hand tenderly. He looks into her eyes, which now had tears welling up in them.

"Aya, you are still beautiful to me, I see a woman, a lady that I would be blessed to call my girl, my woman. I"m here and ready to be with you. I'm open to learning all about pronouns, javora culture, and what you like and don't like, all that.

"Davalii, but loving a woman like me is different. Like what about our sex life, sex with us is different. You know."

So what, I'll learn and figure it out with you.

Ok, what about having children? I can't have children naturally, I'm sure you might want a son. Right?

Yeah maybe, but last time I checked, we are on a island with hundreds of orphans who might need a good home. Adoption could be a real option for us. I'm okay with that too. So what's next?" Davalii says with ease.

Ok, okay um..you know outside and away from the island, the world really don't care for javoras like that. I'm sure you heard about those horrible stories about our murders.

"I know, I know. Now I'll be honest, I might need to get adjusted to that part. But fuck em, I'm still riding with you and ready to stand beside you and fight for you. I won't let nothing happen to you." Davalii says with certainty.

Aya looks in amazement and feels seen, in a new light.

"Davalii are you really like...you're like okay with all of this? Are you sure? You're down for *ME* like this? I just don't know what else to say. I'm speechless right now." Aya says, stuttering with emotions.

"It's okay, then let me talk. Aya since the moment I saw you I knew I would risk it all and give you my all. Hell, I might even start making vegetable deliveries here to the island as my main route. Even travel the world with you. You are worth it. I'm all in. And I'm not saying I know everything about your experience or know all the right things to say, but I'm down for you. Right here with you on the journey." Davalii reassures her.

Tears fall from Aya's eyes like water from her soul. Dropping down over Davalii's shoulders, who is holding and hugging her passionately.

At that moment nothing even matters outside their embrace. Aya suddenly remembered the wise words Ms. Tulsa spoke a few days ago.

"A woman deserves good love too". Aya whispers out loud.

Yes you do. And I'm right here. Davalii says with genuine certainty.

They both held each other for awhile, as time froze and passionate emotions flowed free between them. A new beginning was birthed in this moment, a chance, a risk, a joy, a new sense of life… together.

* * *

The moon was a luminous tan above the dark ocean waters. The island was now packed with locals and visitors all ready for the Moon Welcoming Ceremony to start. The island created a new energy and rhythm with all the drumming from the men visitors. The drummers formed their traditional wide circle leaving an open space in the middle for the women dancers to move freely to the beat. A few women were also drumming and swaying back and forth while others were shaking a brass bell instrument in their hands, each in white and gold loose dresses.

It was tradition to wear white during this particular ceremony to honor the water spirits and to wear something gold to honor their most beloved African deity of the rivers, femininity, and sweetness, the Orisha Oshun. It was an old tradition over hundreds of years, for each Great Mother to honor and embody the Orisha Oshun, only for one night during the drumming of the Moon Welcoming Ceremony. The people could feel a presence of something higher and spiritual as the drumming intensified and dancers flowed in sync with the ocean water. The Great Mother LaRa walks down to the center of the circle wearing a flowing gold dress and a white headwrap with gold crystals across the brim. She also wears a long bracelet and necklace of cowrie shells, exemplifying her African wealth and honoring her people's roots and connection to the mainland. With each step, she hums and sings louder, growing in harmony with the ocean waves and the drums drumming.

The women in the circle started to sing an old African song that speaks about love, honoring the water that's inside us and all around us, and worshiping the great Oshun. The wind started to blow with each step and vibrations of their singing and drumming joined together creating an air ripe for healing, hope and new beginnings. Mother LaRa could feel the grand moment rising so she signaled Layla to come forward out of the crowd to the center of the circle.

Davalii somehow instinctively helps her walk to the center right in front of Mother LaRa.

Mother LaRa smiles down and grabs Layla's hand. With all the commotion from the drumming and ocean waves, she wanted to ensure Layla that she was safe and to relax in her presence.

"It's ok child. Relax and let the music take you to a happy place. You are safe my baby." Great Mother LaRa says smoothly and calmly.

While holding Layla's hand with one hand, she uses her other hand to slowly take out a brass bowl with sparkling water from her dress. Layla looks surprised but still smiles at the beautiful sparking color. Layla can now see two little fish glowing bright blue and swimming in circles around each other. Something so bright and unique she never saw before but was transfixed.

Mother LaRa began singing louder and in a different key than the rest of the dancing women. She sang in beautiful foreign high pitched notes that sounded like the whales in the deep ocean. People can now see some movement and sparking eyes in the nearby water. A few locals stepped back knowing that this moment is rare but also unpredictable. While many of the locals stand in awe and amazement taking in all they were witnessing.

Three mermaids emerged from the shallow waters moving slowly towards Great Mother LaRa.

The mermaids looked straight at Mother LaRa with bright blue sparkling eyes. The mermaids were calm and much larger compared to the myths that most people heard. These mermaids were Black women with long fishtails. One of the mermaids had sparkling gold scales running through the bottom, one had sparkling blue scales in her tail, and the other who remained in the background near the water had blue and white scales in her tail.

Now all the locals and guests stepped way back out of the way in awe. Even the elders who had witnessed these ceremonies for years made space for what was to come next. Gradually, everyone made space in the center of the circle. Only the drummers remained as they continued to beat their drums to the rhythm of the sea.

"Ah Daughter LaRa! Is there a new child on this island?" As the mermaid spoke everyone paid their respect with their silence.

"Yes, Great Mothers of the River and Sea, Yemoja, Oshun, and Olokun. She's a Javora, your rarest and most unique of your children." Mother LaRa's own eyes glowed pure gold as she replied to the mermaids. When this happens, the Great Mother LaRa has ascended to her highest power which is marked by a deep trance, a sign of communication with the higher marine spirits. She has not been fully possessed as she retains the freedom and use of her own voice.

"Is this the Javora child here behind you?" The second Black woman mermaid spoke in a deeper tone, eyes glowing blue and fixed on the young Javora.

"Yes, Great Mothers of the River and Sea. I will call on my daughter to help us with the ritual." Mother LaRa says to the mermaids entranced.

"Aya, my daughter, Princess of the Island of Iza, come help this child with the offering from my garden." Mother LaRa calls out to Aya in the crowd.

Aya who has had many years of experience with these ceremonies, knew what to do and how to continue the sacred ritual.

Aya walked through the crowd almost floating. Her face was illuminated by the bioluminescence flower she carried to give to Layla. The flower glowed a neon blue like diamonds in the night.

Aya gave the following instructions. "Layla, rub this flower all over your skin from head to toe.The flower needs your scent and water from your sweat. Then speak your name into the flower saying these exact words.

"My spirit is one with the water spirits and goddesses. I am a child of the Island of Iza. I am a treasure of the matriarch. The sacred waters will love and protect me."

Layla starts the process of rubbing the glowing flower over her arms and legs. Aya guides her through the entire process. When she was finished, Layla spoke into the flowers,

carefully reciting the narrative given to her by
Aya. Aya helps with soft whispers in her ear.

"Good job Layla, we're almost finished.
Now I néed you to place the flower into the
brass bowl of water and give it to Mother LaRa.
I'm right here beside you. Okay?"

Layla does the action and sees a high
beam of pure light flow through the flower and
the two fishes inside the bowl. She steps closer
to Mother LaRa and the two mermaids and
hands the bowl to Mother LaRa, who takes the
bowl from Layla's hands and smiles warmly at
the Javora-child. She then handed the bowl to
the mermaids closest to her. Both mermaids
began their siren song, a high frequency sound
dedicated to the oceans.

As the three sang, tons of mermaids
raised their heads from the waters almost in
unison. All you could see in the darkness were
their eyes glowing in a rainbow of colors. There
were dozens. The mermaids in the water joined
in the siren song making a majestic sound that
felt as if heaven had descended on earth. A
feeling that took over and filled the hearts of
every human soul.

"Look Layla the mermaids are singing your name! They're singing to welcome you to the island. And always be here to love, guide, and protect you." Aya said to ensure that Layla understood the magnitude of this spiritual moment.

Instinctively, Davalii moved to the front of the crowd. He waved respectfully at both Layla and Aya. The three shared a warm moment together of sheer joy.

The two Black women mermaids lifted the bowl skyward while looking straight at Layla with glowing eyes.

"Welcome my child. We love you and will always be here for you. If you ever need support, just come to the ocean and sing to us for we know your voice and heart. Welcome Home."

The three mermaids smile and look at the islanders around them. Some people were holding hands while others shed tears as pure expressions of a sacred moment in time. Another siren song is released into the wind by all of the mermaids, in perfect harmony. It was a song and language of their own. The three mermaids on land dove back into the waters to join the mothers, with Layla's glowing flower in one of their hands. The Great Mother LaRa returns to her consciousness as the ritual possession becomes less visible in the distance. She slowly regains her composure. The people wave in unison while watching the mermaids dive in the water, swimming in and out the ocean like dolphins. Layla, astonished, whispers to Aya who stands beside her.

"Wow! I can't believe I actually saw mermaids... and they look like me! What are they saying now?" Layla asks, pointing at the mermaids in the distance.

Aya looks at Layla with calm radiant eyes.

"We are all Family. The children of the ocean. Treasures of the Matriarch." Aya says sincerely.

The island is quiet now as residents and guests alike hold hands watching the Mothers of the River & Sea swim in the distance under the watchful moon. The Moon Welcoming Ceremony is complete and Layla has officially been welcomed home. She was now under the protection of the ocean. Aya and Davalii kiss, then hold hands as they watch at the deep blue sea in warm serenity.

Story Glossary & Background
(New Words the Writer Created)

Javora - an island word for transgender or androgynous person. Mostly referring to trans women or feminine people assigned male at birth. (fictional / not a real word)

Island of Iza - a fictional place. One of the islands of Cape Verde, off the coast of Africa. In the story it was bought by a Polynesian King for his new javora wife. An island for javoras women and biological women, also a matriarchal society. Where the story setting is located. (fictional / not a real place)

Mushu - one of the women characters named in the story.

Davalli - one of the men characters named in the story.

Great Mother LaRa- a title of the highest matriarch of the island, a Queen. She is a woman whose role is to govern the island, take care of orphan and homeless children, and lead ceremonies that honor and embody the African Ifa Orishas of the sea and rivers, Yemoja, Oshun, and Olokun. (Fictional / not a real woman who exist)

*** **Please note:** although Cape Verde is a real island and country of Africa, the Island of Iza is not.

*****Please note:** the African deities Oshun, Yemoja, and Olukun are real deities, divine spirits, or Orishas in the pantheon of Ifa/African Spirituality/ African Traditional Religions. However, Mother LaRa is a character in this story, not a real person.

Conversations with Readers

Want to meet the author of this book? Join her on a fun and recorded Zoom call! Read the questions below and send an email to her requesting a Zoom meeting. During the Zoom meeting you will get a chance to discuss the book and answer the questions below. Simply email Ms. Tate here: TheFeminineGardens@gmail.com, please add "Conversations with Readers" in the email subject line.

1. **Self Expression & Advocacy**:

In the first poem tilted *We Are Beautifully Rebellious,* it talks about being a person who is advocating or fighting back in some way. Can you share a moment or time when you had to advocate, fight back, or even have a season of being a rebel in your life? How did you feel during that time?

2. **Sexual Health:**

In the short story called *"The Cat Eyes of Lincoln Drive,"* it's an erotica. Let's explore sexual health for a moment. How comfortable are you with talking to your partner(s) about safer sex, condom / dental dames? Do you all ever discuss getting STI tested regularly?

3. **Sexual Health**:

In the story *"The Cat Eyes of Lincoln Drive"*, Larissa finally gets the sexual desire she has been missing or not getting from her partner. Studies show that sex is actually healthy for our minds and body. Do you feel that sex makes your own mental health better? If so, how?

4. **Wellness through Spirituality**

In the story *"When Love Continues"* Luna talks a lot about past lives and reincarnation. What are your own thoughts on reincarnation? Can you imagine what your past life could've been?

5. **Mental Health**:

In the poem *"Iridescent"*, it talks about honoring and never forgetting the LGBTQ+ Queer trailblazers in history. In your own life, how important is it to have mentors, elders, or inspirational public figures in your life?

6. **Friends and Community**:

In the story *Vibrant,* it shows diverse queer characters as close friends who support each other. How important is friendship, sisterhood, or brotherhood in your own life?

7. **Women's Rights Issues:**

In the poem *Women of my Kind,* it discusses many types of women in the world. Which women's rights issue or social issue should we talk more about or that you are passionate about?

8. **Dating Safety**:

In the story *Treasures of the Matriarch,* Aya decides to share her personal information or disclose a part herself with the guy she's dating, only when she feels safe and comfortable. In your own dating life, what are some dating safety rules that you live by? Why is safety important when dating?

9. **Unique Socialites:**

In the story *"Treasure of the Matriarch"* the story is located in a matriarchal society for women. If you grew up or lived in a matriarchal society, describe that world or what you think would be different from what we see here in America?

10. **Traveling:**

In the story *"Treasures of the Matriarch"* traveling the world is mentioned. What place in the world that you would love to visit or live in?

Bonus: Are there questions you want to ask me about any of the poems or stories?

www.ingramcontent.com/pod-product-compliance
Lightning Source LLC
Chambersburg PA
CBHW071439260626
47170CB00008B/2772